The Magic Water

by Roderick J. Robison

Also by Roderick J. Robison
Middle School Millionaires
The Principal's Son
The Newbie
The Newbie 2
The Lunch Lady's Daughter
The Lunch Lady's Daughter 2
The Christmas Tin

For James

Chapter 1

It was just a cut. Travis Macgregor thought nothing of it. He certainly wasn't about to stop fishing because of it. The laceration on his index finger was not exactly small, but Travis wasn't worried. He had been cut before. He knew about cuts. And he knew the bleeding would stop eventually. What he didn't know though, was that his life was about to change because of *this* cut.

There was nothing really unusual about the cut. Nor was there anything unusual about how Travis had cut his finger. It was the last day of summer vacation. He had been casting along the bank of the river, making his way downstream, when his lure snagged on a submerged log.

The log was just a foot from shore. Travis reached down into the murky water with his right hand to free the lure. And his index finger struck the edge of a broken bottle on the river bed.

After he unhooked the lure from the log, Travis balled his right hand into a fist to stop the blood flow. Then he picked up his spinning rod with his left hand and continued downstream, following a narrow deer trail. The area was covered by a thick blanket of green briers. The deer trail meandered through the dense undergrowth; the going was slow.

Travis continued down the trail toward the cove—his favorite spot. Storm clouds moved in from the west as he bushwhacked his way downstream.

This section of the river was altogether different from the upper reaches that cut through downtown Eastborough. In the downtown area, fishing consisted of sneaking a cast from someone's backyard or casting a lure from the edge of a factory parking lot when nobody was looking. Here though, he had freedom. This area was more reminiscent of Maine's north woods than suburban Massachusetts—except for the distant roar of trucks on the highway and the factory smokestacks that jutted above the tree line.

Because it was so difficult to reach, nobody else ever bothered to make the downstream trek to the cove. Nor did they bother to attempt accessing the cove from the steep, brier-infested ravine that backdropped it. Access by canoe or boat was not possible due to a series of rocks and logs at the mouth of the cove. The cove was all but inaccessible—unless you knew the deer trails that meandered through the dense growth along the riverbank.

Travis knew he'd have the cove to himself. In all the years he'd fished the cove, he had never encountered another angler there. He followed the briar-choked deer trail for ten minutes, squeezing through the undergrowth, thorns ripping into his fishing vest at each turn.

Eventually, the trail brought him to a small point that jutted into the eastern end of the cove. A Great Blue Heron took flight as Travis emerged from the underbrush, a fingerling bass clamped in its beak. A hawk circled high above the ravine behind the cove.

Lily pads dotted the surface of the small unnamed cove. Travis knew Lily pads provided excellent cover for pickerel and bass. He pictured the first strike as he tied a floating lure onto the end of his line. Overhead, the sky continued to darken as storm clouds edged closer. Rain drops dotted the surface of the water as Travis finished tying the lure onto the line.

Winds blew in from the southwest now and bowed the reeds along the perimeter of the cove.

Travis had only made one cast into the cove before the sky unleashed heavy sheets of rain. Wearing just shorts, a t-shirt, and fishing vest, he was ill prepared for the storm. He had not taken notice of the dark clouds in the distance when he left the house that morning. Travis had fishing on his mind.

He reeled in the lure and secured it to the second guide on his spinning rod. Then Travis turned around and started trudging up the trail he had come in on. He cursed himself for not packing a poncho in his fishing vest. The rain was intensifying now, and he was getting soaked!

He hadn't been on the trail but a few minutes when lightening lit up the ravine behind the cove. And that's when Travis spotted it. Just for an instant…A flat rock protruding from the side of the ravine. An overhang. Directly below the rock overhang should be a small patch of dry ground. A place to weather the storm. The overhang was halfway up the ravine.

The sky grew even darker and thunder boomed as Travis headed up the ravine toward the rock overhang. He wrestled his way through the dense undergrowth, getting wetter by the second as briers pricked his legs and arms and tore into his clothing. Lightning lit up the landscape again, providing another snapshot of the rock overhang. He was getting closer.

When Travis finally reached the overhang, he ducked under it, grateful for the dry ground underneath it and the shelter from the rain.

Strange, in all the years he'd fished the cove, he'd never seen the rock overhang before. And then he realized the reason why. Just downhill from the overhang, a felled oak tree stretched across the ravine, the victim of a recent storm. It had been a massive old tree, its upturned roots eerily protruding skyward through the undergrowth. The ancient oak tree had apparently concealed the rock overhang, perhaps for centuries. Travis sat down on the small patch of dry ground directly under the overhang. He stared out into the rain. He couldn't see the river through the driving rain. It was raining that hard. Then the wind shifted; the rain slanted in at him, pelting his body.

The overhang didn't provide quite as much shelter as he had counted on. Travis backed in under the overhang as far as he could, his back against the ravine.

He felt the prick of thorns through the back of his fishing vest. The whole ravine was covered with green briers. Travis turned around to free his vest from the briers...and he noticed a small opening in the ravine just behind him.

At first glance, he took the opening for an animal burrow. But when he carefully pulled the briers away, he saw that the opening was larger than it appeared at first glance. A dark hole in the side of the ravine. It was about four feet high and not quite as wide. Travis peered into the opening. He couldn't see anything inside at first, just inky darkness. Then lightning flashed again and provided him a brief glimpse inside the opening...It was a cave.

In that brief flash, Travis saw glistening rock walls and a shallow pool of crystal clear water at the center of the cave.

Travis brushed aside the rest of the briers that blocked the cave's entrance. Then he stooped down and cautiously stepped into the cave. Once inside, the cave opened up and there was just enough room for him to stand. It took a few moments for his eyes to adjust to the dim light. But soon he could make out the pool in the center of the cave and the glistening walls.

Travis made his way over to the pool and sat down beside it. He couldn't see the far end of the cave, but he'd return with a flashlight the next chance he got—next Saturday. The place would be worth exploring. For now though, he was just glad for the reprieve from the rain. He sat by the pool, staring into the water, listening to the rain thunder down outside.

As he sat there, the injured finger on his right hand started to throb. Travis looked down at the laceration on his index finger. It would be a while before this cut healed, he knew. He dipped his right hand into the pool of water and swished it back and forth to cleanse the cut. The water was surprisingly cool and soothing. He kept his hand in the water for some time.

A little later, he removed the water bottle from his vest and drank the last of his water. Travis then submerged the bottle in the pool and filled it with water. The water could come in handy later on for cleansing the cut. After he filled the bottle, he capped it and placed it back in the front pocket of his fishing vest.

Ten minutes later the rain let up. The storm passed. And the sun came out again in full force. The day wouldn't be a loss after all. There was more fishing to be had.

Travis stepped out of the cave. He squinted at the sunlight. The sunlight was beaming down through the trees now as if nothing had happened. But something had happened. And it wasn't just the storm.

Chapter 2

Travis hung his fishing vest on a hook in the back hall when he got home that afternoon. Then he headed into the bathroom. He grabbed a band-aid from the medicine cabinet and looked down at the cut on his index finger. Travis winced. The cut was worse than he thought. It was *deep*.

He unwrapped the band-aid and gently applied it over the cut. Then he went into the kitchen to grab an apple before starting his paper route. His mother was sitting at the kitchen table looking over the mail—bills. She looked concerned. Travis knew his mother was stressed over their financial situation. It was just the two of them; money was tight. His mother tried to shield Travis from their financial hardships, but he knew what was going on. He saw the *over due* notices, heard his mother on the phone setting up payment plans.

Travis balled his right hand into a fist so his mother wouldn't see the cut. She had enough to worry about.

"Hey, kiddo."

"Hi, Mom."

"…What's wrong with your hand?"

"Huh?"

"You're clenching your right hand." There was no fooling a nurse. His mother didn't miss a trick. The woman had eagle eyes.

"I cut my finger when I was fishing," Travis said. "It's nothing." He knew his mother would want to see the cut and make a big fuss over it if she knew how bad it was. Travis didn't mind the attention. But he didn't have time for it right now. He had papers to deliver.

"Let me take a look at the cut."

Travis winced. "Mom, it's nothing. I've got to go," he said, grabbing an apple from the bowl on the counter. "I'm running late."

His mother frowned. "Okay, but I want to see that cut when you get back. Oh, and I'm working the late shift tonight. I'll leave dinner on the stove for you, sweetheart."

"Thanks, Mom. See you later."

*****

Travis purposely returned later than usual from his paper route. His mother had left for work by the time he got home. He was still awake when she returned from work later that night, though. His mother opened the door to his room and looked in. Travis was in bed. He closed his eyes and pretended he was asleep.

Chapter 3

He woke to the aroma of buttermilk pancakes the following morning.

"Come and get `em while they're hot," his mother called out from the kitchen. Pancakes were a first-day-of-school tradition in the Macgregor family. His mother always prepared a pancake breakfast for him on the first day of school for some reason. She had done so for as long as Travis could remember.

"Morning, Mom." Travis yawned as he stumbled into the kitchen.

"Morning, kiddo." His mother was already dressed in her nursing uniform. "I'm off to work," she said. "Have a good first day."

"Thanks, Mom. And thanks for the pancakes."

"You're welcome, sweetheart. Enjoy."

She was about to leave when she saw the band-aid on his injured finger. "How is the finger?"

Travis downplayed it. "It's fine, just a scratch."

His mother glanced at her watch. He could tell she was debating taking the time to inspect the cut. "All right," she said. "But I want to see that cut later."

"Yes, Mom."

"All right, I'm off. Oh, I'm working a double shift today. Dinner is in the fridge. Tomorrow night we'll have a family meal. You can tell me all about school."

"Sounds good, Mom. Have a good day."

Nobody made pancakes like his mother. But Travis sighed as he sat down to eat his breakfast. It wasn't that he didn't enjoy pancakes. He did. His mother's pancakes were superb. He sighed because the bus would arrive in ten minutes. He had ten minutes to eat, get dressed, brush his teeth, comb his hair, and get to the bus stop. The rush was on. Summer vacation had officially come to an end. Reality was quickly setting in.

*****

There was excitement in the air on the first morning of school at Melven Howard Middle School.

The air was filled with the sounds of slamming lockers and the voices of students catching up with classmates they hadn't seen since school let out back in June. Things settled down though when the students entered their homerooms. Travis soon found out that seventh grade was altogether different than sixth grade.

In sixth grade, the students had spent most of the day in the same classroom, where a two-teacher team taught all of the core subjects. Now there was one teacher for each subject. And each subject was in a different classroom in a different part of the building.

There were just four minutes between classes. It didn't seem like enough time to get to your next class. Travis practically had to run from language arts to pre-algebra, which was at the opposite end of the building. The rushed pace was a stark transition from the dog days of summer. It would take some getting used to. So too would homework. By noon, Travis and his classmates had already been assigned homework in language arts, pre-algebra, and Spanish.

Lunch was almost as rushed as the dash between classes. Then, after lunch came PE, history, and finally, science.

Seventh grade science teacher, Mr. Callahan Calcuttu, was sitting behind his desk reading a newspaper when the seventh period students entered his classroom. He was a short and balding grumpy middle-aged man. The man continued to read the paper for another five minutes after the last student had arrived. It seemed that teaching was cutting into his reading time.

Where the other teachers were well groomed and took pride in their appearance, this guy looked like he'd just rolled out of bed. His thinning hair was tousled. And the man's trousers looked like they had been pulled from a dirty clothes hamper. His shirt was wrinkled too. And there was a coffee stain on his loose-knotted tie. From the look on his face, it appeared the guy didn't want to be there any more than the students. Unlike his fellow teachers who had spent the summer running day camps, teaching summer school, or working seasonal jobs, this guy had spent his summer cooped up in his apartment where he slept until noon each day. His afternoons were spent watching *get rich* infomercials on the television. Over the course of the summer, he had responded to just about every *get rich* promotion that came along. The guy was always looking to make a quick buck—without having to work for it. He'd tried dozens of get-rich-quick schemes. And he'd never earned a penny from any of them. Still, he was always on the lookout for an easy buck to supplement his salary.

Mr. Calcuttu finally stopped reading and put the newspaper down on his desk. Then he slowly took attendance. After that, he handed out a class schedule and distributed text books. After each student had received a text book, he instructed the class to read the first chapter. Then he went back to his desk, picked up his newspaper, and continued with his reading.

Travis started to read his text book, but his mind wandered. It had been a long day. And a big adjustment from the freedom of summer. He glanced down at his right hand and looked his injured index finger. Travis flexed the finger. Surprisingly, there was no pain, no soreness. And he recalled that the injury hadn't even bothered him during rope climbing in PE that afternoon. *Strange.*

Just before the dismissal bell, Mr. Calcuttu put down his paper and said, "Listen up, people. You have a homework assignment."

This brought a number of groans. The students already had enough homework as it was.

"Relax, people. It's not a demanding assignment."

Mr. Calcuttu handed each student a 3"x5" index card and told the class, "Your homework is to choose a science project. All seventh-graders are required to complete a science project. The project will be due on October 15th. Each project will be put on display in the hallway outside our classroom. We do this each year; it's nothing new."

"You'll find the criteria listed on the class website. You need to write your name and the name of your project on the card. You'll turn the cards in to me a week from Friday. And please, people—no *volcanoes*. They're getting old."

Brriiiiinngg!

Science class had come to an end. And so too had the first day of school. Travis had no idea what he'd do for his project. He was just glad school was over for the day.

Chapter 4

The bundle of papers was on the front stoop when he got home that afternoon. Just like always. Travis went inside the house and dropped his backpack off in his room. Then he went to the kitchen to grab a quick snack. After that, he loaded the papers into the delivery bag, strapped the bag over his left shoulder, and headed out the door.

*****

He returned from the paper route at five o'clock and ate dinner alone at the kitchen table. After dinner, he did homework and watched some television. When his mother pulled her rusted fifteen-year-old sedan into the driveway later that night, Travis turned off the television and headed to his room. Like the night before, he pretended to be asleep when his mother checked in on him. Once again, he avoided having to show her the deep cut on his index finger.

*****

Travis sat through language arts, pre-algebra, and Spanish the next morning. He went through the motions. He listened, took notes, wrote down homework assignments, and even asked a few questions. But that afternoon, history class was different. He was very attentive in history. History was Travis's favorite subject, always had been.

The history teacher, Mrs. Tibbets, was covering the customs of Native American Indians in Pre-Colonial America. Travis paid attention to every detail.

That afternoon, Mrs. Tibbets concentrated on the tribes of the northeast woodlands. She informed the students that over the summer she had worked with an archaeological team uncovering an old Indian settlement in the western part of the state.

"The area you live in now," she told the class, "was home to the Wampanoags. The Wampanoags lived in wigwams. They fished the local river and cleared land to plant corn and squash. They also

19

harvested raspberries, blueberries and wild game from the woodlands."

She went on to tell the students how the Wampanoags survived through cold winters and hot summers. Then she said, "The area to the west of us, in what is now New York, was home to another tribe— the Mohawks. It has been said that the Mohawks and the Wampanoags were enemies. The Mohawks lived in longhouses—long wood-frame buildings sheathed with bark. Sometimes, more than a hundred people lived together in these dwellings. And the Mohawks also planted corn, squash and other crops. And they too harvested berries, fish and game."

"For your homework assignment tonight," Mrs. Tibbets said, "you will research the customs and traditions of the Wampanoags and the Mohawks. And you'll write a one-page summary of the differences between the two tribes."

Some students groaned, but Travis was not among them. He looked forward to *this* homework assignment.

*****

The paper route went smoothly that afternoon. The dog that usually chased him down Mill Lane was chained to a yard stake for once. The traffic wasn't bad. And the weather was cooperative.

Travis finished the route in time to join in on a street hockey game down at the vacant lot by the intersection of Main Street and Pleasant Street. He played street hockey for forty-five minutes, then headed home for dinner.

When he got home, there was a note from his mother on the kitchen table:

Working late again.
Dinner is on stove.

Travis ate dinner in silence once again. Then he watched television for an hour. After that he took a shower. Then he headed to his room and studied up on the customs and traditions of the Wampanoags and the Mohawks. He read the handout that Mrs. Tibbets had distributed in class that day. And he did some research online as well. Then he wrote a one-page report on the differences between the two tribes.

His eyelids grew heavy as he finished the report. Travis yawned. Sleep came quickly; he was out like a light by nine o'clock. And he began to dream...

Chapter 5

Autumn 1558

Mist rose off the tea-colored river in the gray light of early dawn. Upstream, a birchbark canoe rounded the riverbend. The canoe was barely perceptible at first as it drifted slowly downriver into the mist. Then, six men materialized inside the canoe. Wampanoag warriors.

The warrior in the stern held a paddle, as did the warrior in the bow. The other four men scanned the riverbank. All six of them were weary; they had traveled far. Some of the men were bleeding from lacerations on their arms and chest. All of them were bruised. Battle with the Mohawks had taken its toll.

The sun began to rise as the canoe continued downstream. Colorful foliage lined the riverbanks. The canoe passed by a fish weir and a series of beaver dams.

The skilled paddlers maneuvered the canoe around a series of treacherous rocks at the mouth of a cove. Then they paddled across the smooth waters of the cove toward the far shore. The far shoreline was backdropped by a ravine.

When the canoe reached the shoreline, the warrior in the bow hopped out and steadied it. The others slowly disembarked. A few of the warriors were limping and had to be assisted by those with less severe wounds. Two of the more able-bodied warriors pulled the canoe up onto the beach.

Among the warriors was a medicine man. He led the way up the ravine through dense briers. The others slowly trailed after him single-file. They followed a game trail that meandered up the ravine. It brought them to a small opening in the side of the ravine. A cave.

There was a small oak tree in front of the cave's entrance. The medicine man brushed some branches aside, then stooped down, and stepped into the cave. The others followed him into the cave.

Water glistened on the walls of the cave. And there was a pool of crystal clear water at the center of the cave. The warriors sat down beside the pool. Those that could dipped their wounded hands, arms and legs into the cool water. The medicine man ladled water over the cuts of the more severely injured. He carefully soaked lacerations, bruises, swollen ankles and other wounds with the water.

The party camped in the cave that night. The following day, there was much improvement in the warriors' health. To pass the time, some of the warriors made flint arrowheads on a flat rock at the back of the cave. Others repaired bows and patched torn buckskin clothing.

Two days after they arrived, the six Wampanoags stepped out of the cave. It was as if none of them had suffered an injury. All of the warriors were able-bodied now; none of them limped.

They walked down the ravine and made their way to the beach, where they dragged the canoe to the water's edge. Then the six warriors hopped into the canoe and paddled off to their village, their strength regained.

Brriiiiinngg!

Travis rolled over and stared at the alarm clock. It read 6:45AM. The dream was still vivid in his mind. It had been so realistic.

His mother was sitting at the kitchen table when he stepped into the kitchen for breakfast. She glanced at the band-aid on his injured finger.

"Okay," she said. "Let me see that cut."

"Mom, it's nothing."

His mother's eyebrows lifted. "Have a seat. This won't take but a minute."

Travis sighed. There was no avoiding it. He sat down beside his mother.

Here we go.

Travis slowly removed the band-aid. He knew his mother would not be happy when she saw the size of the cut. He braced himself for the worst. He winced as he removed the band-aid...but there was no cut— just a very thin, faint white line where the cut had been. It was barely perceptible. *Huh?*

"I guess you were right about the cut," his mother said, tousling his hair. "Doesn't look like it was that bad after all. It healed very quickly too, I might add."

Travis was baffled. He recalled how big the cut had been, remembered the depth of the laceration. None of his other cuts had ever healed so quickly. And the other cuts hadn't been nearly as deep. He didn't have time to dwell on it, though. He had a bus to catch.

*****

His dream had retreated to the far reaches of his mind by first period that morning. It wasn't until seventh period that he thought about it again. Mr. Calcuttu had instructed the students to read the second chapter in their textbook. Travis's thoughts wandered. He stared at his index finger on his right hand and looked at the faint, paper-thin scar where the cut had been. He thought about some of his previous cuts. The last one had taken a long time to heal, the one before that even longer. And those cuts had been much smaller. *Strange*.

It was at that moment that the dream came back to him…and the pool of water in the cave that had healed the Wampanoag warriors. Travis couldn't help but wonder…was it the water in the cave that had miraculously healed his cut so quickly?

He wanted to explore the cave more than ever now. Travis couldn't wait for Saturday. Saturday was two days away. An eternity.

Chapter 6

When he stepped into the kitchen for breakfast on Saturday morning, his mother was sitting at the table. Travis's eyebrows lifted when he saw that his mother's left foot was propped up on a footstool. Her left ankle was swollen—it was twice the size of her right ankle. A pair of crutches leaned against the wall beside her.

"Mom, what happened?"

"Oh, I twisted my ankle in the parking lot at work yesterday. I guess I was in too much of a hurry."

"Can I get you anything?"

"No, sweetheart. There's not much that can be done. The doctor said I need to keep my foot elevated. I'm not to walk on it for a week."

"Sorry, Mom."

"Thanks, kiddo."

*****

Travis stashed his bike in the woods at the river's edge. Then he headed down the trail that cut into the woodland. He carried a flashlight and a bucket this time rather than a fishing rod.

The trail soon turned muddy and then the woods gave way to swamp. The swamp was dotted with clumps of marsh grass. Travis crisscrossed the swamp, jumping from one clump of marsh grass to another, attempting to keep his feet dry.

After clearing the swamp, he entered more woodland. The forest floor was blanketed with green briers now. Travis made his way downstream, following a deer trail that meandered through the thick undergrowth. He reached the cove a half hour after ditching his bike.

When he reached the cove's far shore, he headed up into the ravine. There wasn't a cloud in the sky, but the forest was dark underneath the canopy of thick trees. There was an eeriness to the place. It was no wonder that nobody but him visited this place.

Travis got turned around a few times in the dense growth. But after ten minutes of bushwhacking, he spotted the rock overhang. He heard the sound of heavy construction equipment—bulldozers and

29

backhoes—in the distance. The land above the ravine was being cleared for development—a residential subdivision. Travis had seen construction equipment and the new subdivision sign on his paper route the day before.

It took him another five minutes to make his way up to the cave. Once there, he brushed away the briers from the entrance and turned on his flashlight. Then he stooped down and entered the cave. The walls glistened with trails of water that seeped down from above. And the pool of water was there just like he remembered—just like in his dream.

Travis pointed the flashlight at the pool of water. The water was still crystal clear. The sound of water dripping onto rock could be heard from the back of the cave. Travis focused the flashlight's beam at the back of the cave. Just before the far wall was a large flat rock. He pointed the flashlight at the rock and made his way over to it.

Moving closer, Travis noticed chips of a different type of rock on top of it. He picked one of the chips up. Its jagged surface was surprising smooth. The rock chip was triangular in shape. Looking closer, he saw that it was an arrowhead.

There were two other arrowheads on top of the rock as well. And the ground surrounding the rock was strewn with smaller chips of what Travis guessed to be flint. He started to collect the arrowheads, but something inside him told him not to and he left them where they lay.

He then made his way over to the pool. Travis dipped the bucket in the pool and filled it to the brim. Then he carried the bucket outside, squinting as his eyes adjusted to the daylight.

Amazingly, very little water spilled from the bucket on the long and treacherous trek back to his bike. When Travis reached his bike, he looped the handle of the bucket over the Schwinn's handlebars and headed home.

His mother was still sitting at the kitchen table when he got home. She was rubbing ointment on her swollen left ankle.

"Hey, Mom."

His mother's face brightened when she saw him. "Hi, kiddo. What's in the bucket?"

"Something for your foot."

"Water?" his mother observed.

31

"Water for an experiment," Travis said. "An experiment that I need your help with."

"Sure thing. How can I be of assistance?"

Travis placed the bucket on the floor in front of his mother. "Just dip your left foot in the water—and soak your ankle."

His mother's eyebrows arched. "Is there something you're not telling me?"

Travis grinned. "It's just an experiment. I don't know anything—yet."

His mother smiled and lowered her left foot into the bucket. Her ankle was completely submerged in the water.

"It's quite cool...and soothing. How long should I soak my ankle for?" his mother inquired.

"As long as you like."

Travis headed off to deliver papers.

When he returned from the paper route, his mother was still sitting at the kitchen table. She was on the phone, talking to her sister. Her left ankle was still submerged in the bucket of water. It wasn't likely she would be getting up anytime soon. His mother and aunt sometimes talked on the phone for hours.

32

*****

Travis woke to the sound of humming on Sunday morning. The air in the house was tinged with the aroma of fresh paint. When he stepped out of his room, Travis saw his mother painting the hallway wall. He blinked and rubbed the sleep out of his eyes to be sure he wasn't dreaming. But it was no dream. His mother was humming a tune in sync with the radio. She was standing there as if her left ankle had never bothered her.

"Good morning, sunshine."

"You're standing," Travis said. "You're ankle is okay?"

"Never better," his mother chirped. "I woke up pain-free. It must've been that long soak in the water you brought me yesterday. I think it was just what I needed!"

"That's great, Mom!"

Travis smiled. But his smile quickly disappeared when his mother said, "Grab a roller and give me a hand."

"By the way. Did you put something in the water?" His mother asked.

Travis shook his head. "No, nothing at all."

"It was just plain old water? Tap water?"

Travis smiled. "No. The water is from a cave I found down by the river when I was fishing."

"Well, I'll be."

Chapter 7

Monday was the busiest day on the paper route. It was collection day; the day Travis collected the weekly payments from his customers. He was running later than usual when he reached the last stop on his route—the Riverview Nursing Home.

There was just one customer there—a spry eighty-seven-year-old woman named Iris Calhoune. The woman was a bundle of energy. She was a retired school teacher.

Though she was a resident at the nursing home, you wouldn't know it looking at her. She was not one to stay idle. The woman helped other residents with various things around the nursing home. And she helped the kitchen staff too. Iris Calhoune often worked side-by-side with the kitchen staff, preparing meals. She baked cookies as well. And she always offered Travis a cookie when she saw him. She had quickly become his favorite customer.

As he entered the front vestibule and made his way down the hallway to Iris's room, Travis wondered what type of cookie she would offer him. He passed by the entertainment room, where a dozen residents were sitting around the television. Most were clad in bathrobes and pajamas. A few were sitting in wheelchairs; others utilized walkers. Travis was continually amazed at the difference between Iris and the other residents. Though she was their age, she had far more energy, it seemed. And the woman took great pride in her appearance. Her clothing contrasted sharply with the bed clothes that most of the other residents wore.

When he arrived at her room, Travis was not surprised to see that Iris was wearing a vibrant red silk blouse and a dark woolen skirt. But he *was* surprised to see that she wasn't smiling. The woman seemed a bit sad, in fact. Travis had never seen Iris like this before. The woman was always so upbeat.

"Hello, Mrs. Calhoune."

"Oh, hi there, Travis."

Travis placed the paper on her nightstand as the woman rummaged through her purse for her payment envelope. She seemed a bit distracted as she extracted the payment envelope and handed it to Travis.

"Are you okay?" Travis asked her.

Iris Calhoune furrowed her brow. "Oh, I'm sorry to be like this, Travis. It's my hands. They're arthritic. They have been troubling me so. It seems I'm not much help in the kitchen in this condition. I dropped a platter of food yesterday. And I'm not able to bake. I'm sorry. I'm unable to offer you any cookies today."

"Nothing to be sorry about," Travis replied. "I'm sorry to hear about your pain."

'Thanks. Don't mind this old lady." Iris finally flashed a smile.

"Well, see you tomorrow, Mrs. Calhoune."

"Goodbye, Travis. You are the highlight of my day, I'll have you know."

Travis smiled. "Thanks."

An idea came to him on the way home—an idea for another *experiment*. Tomorrow, Tuesday, was an early release day at school. He'd have just enough time to make it back to the cave tomorrow afternoon.

Chapter 8

The nursing coordinator was on the phone at the front desk when Travis arrived at the nursing home late the following afternoon. She smiled and waved at him as he walked past the front desk. And her eyebrows lifted when she noted that he was carrying a bucket of water.

Travis glanced inside the entertainment room on his way down the hall. The usual dozen patrons were clustered around the television. And he was surprised to see Iris Calhoune among them. This was a first. And Iris was wearing a bathrobe—another first.

Travis set the bucket of water down in the hallway, against the wall where nobody would trip over it. Then he stepped into the entertainment room and walked over to Iris.

"Hi, Mrs. Calhoune. How are you?"

Iris diverted her attention from the television. She smiled for the first time that day. "Oh, hello there, Travis."

"Um…I brought you something."

Iris looked at him questioningly. "Oh?"

"Yes…something for your hands. I could leave it in your room if you like."

"Well, that's very kind of you. Perhaps you could escort me down to my room and show me what it is that you brought me. You have my curiosity."

"You bet."

Iris said goodbye to her friends. She and Travis headed out into the hallway. Once there, Travis reached down and picked up the bucket of water.

"Is that for the plants?" Iris inquired, as they made their way down the hall.

"No…actually, this water is for you."

"For me?"

"It's for your hands."

Iris seemed baffled. "I'm sorry…you lost me."

"I brought the water so you can soak your hands in it," Travis explained. "My mother had a sore ankle the other day. Her ankle was much better after she soaked it in this water."

"This is the *same* water that your mother soaked her ankle in?"

"No, it's not the *actual* water she soaked her ankle in. But it's from the same source."

"Oh, well, that sounds good to me. It's very nice of you to think of me. How lucky I am to have such a thoughtful paperboy—and friend."

"My pleasure."

When they reached Iris's room, Travis looked around for a suitable place to leave the water. A place where it would be within easy reach. The nightstand beside Iris's bed caught his eye. Travis placed the bucket of water on the nightstand. Then he said, "See you tomorrow, Mrs. Calhoune. I hope your hands feel better."

Iris smiled. "See you then, my friend. Thanks again for your thoughtfulness."

Chapter 9

Iris Calhoune wasn't in her room when Travis stopped by to deliver her paper the following day. But she was there on Thursday afternoon. When Travis knocked on her door that afternoon he heard a cheerful reply: "I'm coming!"

Iris opened the door a few seconds later. She was dressed in a cashmere sweater and wool slacks. And she was smiling. Resting on the nightstand was a tray of freshly-baked sugar cookies. "Hello, Travis. Good to see you!"

"Hi, Mrs. Calhoune."

Iris picked up the tray of cookies from the nightstand and handed it to him. "I tried a new recipe today. Tell me what you think."

Travis picked up a cookie from the tray and took a bite. "Delicious."

Iris beamed. "I'm glad you like them. I'll wrap them up for you. You can share them with your mother."

"Thanks!"

"It's the least I can do."

Travis glanced down at the woman's hands. "Your hands are better?"

"I am pain-free. And I owe it all to you, Travis. Whatever it was in that water seems to have healed my hands. The kitchen staff was glad to see me back."

"I'm glad."

Iris placed the cookies in a small cardboard container and handed it to him. "Enjoy."

"Thanks, Mrs. Calhoune. I will. See you later."

"See you, my friend. And thanks so much again."

Travis flashed a smile. "Anytime."

Chapter 10

"Okay, everyone," Mr. Calcuttu announced to the class on Friday afternoon. "The science project topics are due. Time to hand in your index cards."

Most of the students were prepared and had selected a science project. Travis was among them.

After he collected all of the index cards, Mr. Calcuttu began to read them to the class. "A solar oven," he announced as he reviewed the first index card in the stack. "That's acceptable."

Next was a soil permeability experiment. After that was a homemade weather station. The science teacher deemed those projects acceptable too. Then he picked up the next index card from the stack. "A *cave?*" he asked. "That's the best you could come up with, Mr. Macgregor?"

Travis winced…and then an idea came to him. "Yes. It won't be an ordinary cave, though."

The science teacher chuckled. "No? Please elaborate."

Travis hesitated a moment. Then he said, "The cave will have a special feature."

"A *special feature* you say? What might that be?"

"There will be a pool of water inside the cave."

Mr. Calcuttu rolled his eyes. "So what! What do you think is so special about a pool of water inside a cave, Mr. Macgregor?"

Travis gulped. Then he said, "The water in the pool will have a special quality...It will be healing water. Water that can cure certain ailments and—"

"Stop," the science teacher interrupted. "If I were you, I'd reconsider and choose something else. Your proposed cave is hovering on the borderline of unacceptable. It's right up there with *volcanoes*. But if you're set on a *cave*, so be it. The next project is a…"

*****

Travis worked on his science project in his spare time during the weeks that followed. He started with a 2' x 2' piece of plywood. He painted the plywood gray. Then he purchased some clay from the hobby shop downtown and molded it into a cave.

He modeled the cave after the actual cave in the ravine behind the cove. Travis constructed the cave to scale as best he could. He wiped olive oil on the inside walls to give them a glistening effect. And he glued leaves and small bits of briers around the outside of the cave to make it as realistic as possible. Once the cave was competed, Travis mounted it on the plywood base.

The next step was to construct a pool at the center of the cave. Travis placed a small tin in the center of the cave. Then he built up the floor around the tin with clay so that the cave's floor was level with the top edge of the tin. After that he pressed fine gravel into the cave's floor to make it look as look as natural as possible.

Next, using a flashlight bulb, two wires and a battery, Travis jerry rigged a small light inside the cave. He wired a small push-button for the light, just outside the cave's entrance.

The final step was to add water to the artificial pool inside the cave. Travis considered just using tap water. But he figured since he had come this far, he might as well do things right and obtain some actual water from the real cave in the ravine. And so, on the first Saturday of October, he ventured down to the river and made his way to the cave once more and filled a bottle with water from the pool in the cave.

Chapter 11

On the morning of October 15th Travis's mother dropped him off at school on her way to work. He carried his science project to the science wing and placed it on the display shelf in the hallway outside Mr. Calcuttu's classroom. Mr. Calcuttu had instructed the students to place their science projects on the shelf when they arrived at school that day. He informed them that their projects would be on display for the next month.

After placing the cave on the display shelf, Travis removed a water bottle from his backpack, removed the lid, and filled the artificial pool inside the cave with water from the real cave. Once the pool was filled, he mounted a small sign by the cave's entrance. It was the size of a business card. The sign read: MAGIC WATER. There was an arrow below the wording. It pointed to the pool of water inside the cave. After the sign was in place, Travis tested the light to be sure it worked. Then he went to his homeroom.

*****

Mr. Calcuttu was reading the newspaper at his desk—as usual—when the students arrived for seventh period that afternoon. After the last student arrived, he put his newspaper down on his desk and said: "Each of you will provide a brief overview of your project today. Let's move out to the hallway."

When all of the students were in the hallway, Mr. Calcuttu walked to the right end of the display shelf. The first project was Todd Ackerman's homemade weather station. Todd reviewed the components of the weather station: a glass jar barometer, wind vane, and rain gauge. The wind vane and the rain gauge were pretty self-explanatory, but Todd went into some details about the construction of the glass jar barometer with its stick pointer.

Next up was Sarah Cauldir's soil permeability experiment. The experiment involved three different types of soil. Sarah reviewed a chart and talked about "perk times." She also discussed which types of soil were best for growing crops.

After that, Jennifer McNairey talked about her solar oven and benefits of cooking with solar heat. When Jennifer finished, Mr. Calcuttu said, "Travis Macgregor. You're up. Tell us about this…cave."

Travis cleared his throat. "Well," he began. "This cave is modeled after an actual cave here in Eastborough. I tried to make it to scale as best I could."

Travis pushed the light button. Inside the cave, the walls glistened and the water in the pool sparkled. The students gathered around to take a look inside the cave.

"One at a time," announced Mr. Calcuttu. "Everyone will get a chance to see it. Continue, Mr. Macgregor."

Travis had done some research on caves. He discussed stalactites and stalagmites. And he talked about how caves are formed. Travis told the class how he used olive oil to make the interior walls shine, just like the real cave. He was almost finished when Davis Trente cut in.

"What's up with the *magic water*?" Davis asked, pointing to the small sign beside the cave's entrance.

Travis cleared his throat again. "The water inside the cave is...therapeutic. It heals certain ailments."

"Yeah right!" Davis scoffed.

"Fat chance," Mr. Calcuttu mumbled.

Travis shrugged. "It's true."

Mr. Calcuttu rolled his eyes. Then he said, "Next!" Everyone continued down the hallway to the next science project on the display shelf.

Chapter 12

The following afternoon, Mr. Calcuttu stopped by the teacher's lounge for a cup of coffee. A group of teachers were sitting at a table in the center of the room eating lunch. As the science teacher was filling his mug with coffee, the art teacher asked, "How are the science projects looking this year, Cal?"

Mr. Calcuttu looked over at the woman. "Well, there are no *volcanoes* this year. That's a plus. I'm so tired of volcanoes." Then the man chuckled to himself. "Of course, one student constructed a *cave*."

"A cave?" the art teacher asked.

Mr. Calcuttu smirked. "That's right. A cave—with a pool of *magic water*. The student that made the project thinks the water has special healing abilities. Now I've heard them all."

The art teacher laughed. So too did Mr. Calcuttu and the other teachers—everyone that is, except for the music teacher, Mrs. Audreye. She was the oldest among the group. The woman had been a talented pianist. She had played the piano for each school play and concert...until this year. Her left wrist was bothering her as of late. The sounds of piano music could no longer be heard in the hallway outside her classroom.

After school that day, Mrs. Audreye slowly made her way down the hallway to the science wing. Once there, she stopped at the display shelf outside Mr. Calcuttu's classroom. She walked slowly by the shelf, taking in a homemade weather station, a soil permeability display, and a solar oven. Then she stopped when she came to the fourth exhibit. A cave.

Mrs. Audreye studied the clay-molded cave. Then she stared at the small sign beside the cave's entrance. The sign that read: MAGIC WATER. She pushed the light button and glanced inside the cave, took in the glistening walls...and the pool of water at the center of the cave.

The woman glanced up and down the hallway. When she was sure there was nobody around, she tentatively reached her left hand inside the cave. The opening was just wide enough to reach her hand through. She reached in up to her elbow. The pool of water was just large enough to accommodate both her hand and her wrist. She soaked her left hand and wrist in the pool.

The water was cool and soothing. It felt good. The woman was in no hurry to leave.

Chapter 13

Iris Calhoune had a visitor in her room when Travis stopped by to deliver her paper that afternoon. The two of them were drinking tea.

"Oh, hi there Travis," Iris said, when he knocked on her door. "Come in, come in. This is my friend, Burt Baskis. He lives down the hall."

"Nice to meet you, Burt."

"Hello, young man. Good to meet you too." The guy was about to shake hands with Travis when he stopped and winced in pain. Then he rubbed his right elbow.

"Burt's elbow has been bothering him," Iris said.

"Indeed," Burt confirmed. "I fell a while back. And my elbow has been bothering me ever since. Can't play tennis anymore." The man was eighty-five-years-old and had still played tennis several times a week right up until his injury.

"Burt's stubborn," Iris said. "He refuses to see the doctor."

Burt grinned. "I see the doctor often enough as it is."

A thoughtful look crossed Iris's face just then. "Travis…I hate to impose on you. But, do you suppose you might be able to bring Burt some of that water you brought me? Perhaps it would help his elbow."

Travis smiled. "Sure. You bet."

Burt's eyebrows lifted. "*Water?*"

Iris smiled. "Trust me."

"Okay."

"I could bring the water on Saturday," Travis offered.

"That would be swell. Thank you, Travis."

"No problem."

*****

When Mrs. Audrey woke up Wednesday morning, she sensed something was different. Something had changed. But she couldn't pinpoint what it was.

She prepared for her day and went about her business. The woman arrived at school at seven-thirty that morning. She stopped by the teacher's lounge, placed her lunch in the refrigerator, and poured herself a cup of coffee. Then she went to her classroom.

The janitor had returned six music stands that had been used for a recent event in the auditorium. He had left them lined up against the front wall of the classroom. They were in the way and would have to be relocated to the back of the room. Mrs. Audreye winced at the thought of moving the music stands. Lifting them would result in a throbbing pain in her left wrist, she knew.

She made her way over to the music stands, dreading the task of relocating them. *Might as well get it over with.*

Mrs. Audreye tentatively picked up a music stand…and there was no pain in her left wrist.

Chapter 14

Travis woke earlier than usual on Saturday morning. After a quick breakfast, he went to the garage and grabbed a bucket. He looped it over the Schwinn's handlebars and headed to the river.

The hardwoods in the ravine were in their fall splendor now. From a distance, the ravine looked like an artist's palette of mixed reds, yellows and oranges. And the weeds along the riverbank had transitioned from green to gold. But the briers were still the same shade of green. And they tore into Travis's clothing as he made his way through the woods.

When he reached the cave, the water in the pool was crystal clear, just like it had been the day he discovered the cave. Travis filled the bucket to the brim. Then he stepped out of the cave and headed down the ravine with the bucket of water, doing his best not to spill any of the precious water.

*****

He delivered the papers in reverse order that day to avoid having to lug the bucket of water the whole time. He stopped by the nursing home first. The nursing coordinator was on the phone at the front desk when he arrived. Her eyebrows shot up when she saw he was carrying another bucket of water.

Travis didn't know which room Burt lived in, so he made his way down the hall to Iris's room. He knocked on Iris's door but she was not home. Travis placed her paper and the bucket of water on the floor in the hallway, just outside her room.

*****

On Monday morning, the janitor at Melven Howard Middle School was replacing a light bulb in the hallway. It was still early; the students hadn't arrived yet. The man liked this time of the day, the quiet time before the first bell.

He was standing on a stepladder, finishing up, when he heard piano music. It had been a long time since the man had heard piano music. It was emanating from just down the hallway.

The janitor stepped down from the stepladder and walked down the hall. He ended up in front of the music room. He glanced inside the room.

Mrs. Audreye was playing the piano. And she was humming the lyrics to the song she was playing. There was a smile on the woman's face.

The janitor stood there for a few minutes, absorbed in the pleasant music. And when Mrs. Audreye finished, he clapped profusely.

The music teacher turned around. She blushed when she saw the janitor standing in the doorway.

"Bravo!" said the janitor. "I have missed your music."

"Well, thank you. It's good to be back!"

When the first period students arrived in Mrs. Audreye's classroom that morning, they were treated to a piano repertoire. It was a most welcome change. Mrs. Audreye's piano playing was the talk of the school that day.

In the teacher's lounge, during lunch that afternoon, the teachers praised Mrs. Audreye, told her how enjoyable it was to hear piano music in the hallways once again.

"Did you have surgery on your hand?" one of the teachers asked Mrs. Audreye.

Mrs. Audreye shook her head no. "No, nothing like that...I...uh...was admiring one of the science projects in the science wing last week...The cave exhibit....I dipped my wrist in the pool of water inside the cave. There must've been something in that water. My wrist feels wonderful now."

Mr. Calcuttu was sitting at the table. He was about to bite into a baloney and mustard sandwich. *Huh?*

Chapter 15

Mr. Calcuttu approached Travis the moment he stepped into the classroom that afternoon. "Mr. Macgregor, good to see you!"

"Uh…thanks, Mr. Calcuttu."

"I'd like to talk to you. Can you stick around after class?"

Travis shrugged. "Sure, I guess so."

"Splendid!"

*****

Iris was seated at her usual table in the nursing home's cafeteria eating a late lunch with her friend, Eleanor. The two of them were chatting when they heard whistling. They looked over toward the cafeteria's entrance. Burt Baskis was walking toward them. He was smiling. They could not remember the last time they'd seen the guy in such a good mood.

"Good afternoon, ladies!" Burt boomed.

"Hello, Burt," said Iris. "What got into you today? I can't recall the last time I saw you in such good spirits. Did you have a special visitor today? Or did you win the lottery?"

"Neither," Burt replied. "It's my elbow. It feels fantastic! Tennis anyone?"

Eleanor's eyebrows arched. "That was a pretty quick recovery, Burt. I saw how much pain you were in last week."

"Well, thanks to that *water*, I'm pain-free now. That water healed my elbow I tell you."

"*Water*?" Eleanor said.

"That's right," Burt smiled. "It was water that healed my elbow. *Special water*. Iris's paperboy brought it."

"Is that so?"

Iris nodded. "Burt's right," she confided. "That water healed my hands. I'm back to baking and helping the kitchen crew again."

"Where did your paperboy get this water *from*?"

Iris shrugged. "Don't know. I didn't ask."

"Well, I could sure use some of that water for my arthritis," Eleanor commented.

"Me too!" said a man at the table next to them.

"Same here!" shouted someone from another table.

"I want some of that water!"

Word had obviously spread quickly from table to table. And soon, even those at the farthest tables had heard about the water. There was excitement in the air. And everyone in the cafeteria wanted some of the water.

*****

"So, now you all know about photosynthesis," Mr. Calcuttu concluded.

Travis yawned. The science teacher had droned on for forty minutes about light, energy, proteins, chloroplasts, and a dozen other things. The guy had never been so enthusiastic.

Brriiiiinngg!

Finally. Travis was thankful for the bell. He couldn't wait to leave. But Mr. Calcuttu was hovering by the doorway. "Mr. Macgregor," he announced, as Travis was about to exit the room. "I'd like to have a word with you."

Travis stopped. He furrowed his brow. "Oh yeah."

Mr. Calcuttu raised his hands. "Don't worry. You haven't done anything wrong. It's all good. I'd like to discuss your project."

"Okay."

After the rest of the students had departed and it was just the two of them, Mr. Calcuttu said, "You'll be glad to know that you're getting an *A* on your project."

Travis gulped. He hadn't expected this.

"I'd like to hear about the inspiration behind the cave. You mentioned there is a cave here in Eastborough?" the science teacher inquired. There was an eagerness in the guy's voice. And there was a kind of desperate look in his eyes.

Travis hesitated for a moment. Then he said, "That's right."

"And there is a pool of water in this cave?"

Travis nodded. "Yes sir. I used the water from the pool in the cave for my project."

Mr. Calcuttu pointed to Travis's science project on the shelf out in the hallway. "Why do you call the water *magic*?"

"Well," Travis said. "The water seems to heal certain ailments."

The science teacher's eyes grew wide. "Please elaborate."

"There's not much to tell, really. I cut my finger. The cut was pretty deep. And I soaked it in the water. The cut healed very fast after that." Travis raised his right hand and showed the science teacher the faint line on his index finger where the cut had been.

Mr. Calcuttu's eyes widened again. "Anything else?"

"Yes. The water healed my mother's ankle, too. One day she was using crutches and the next day she was pain free after soaking her ankle in the water."

"Has anyone besides you or your mother had an ailment healed by the water?"

"Yes," Travis replied. "One of the customers on my paper route. She was having trouble with her hands. So I brought her a bucket of water from the cave. And she's pain free now too."

"Very interesting. Very interesting, indeed. Thank you, Mr. Macgregor. You are dismissed. I hope you didn't miss your bus."

"No problem. I can take the late bus if I did," Travis said.

Mr. Calcuttu was usually the first teacher out the door at the end of the school day. But today was an exception. He waited in his classroom until all of the other teachers and administrators had left. It was just past five o'clock when he stepped out into the hallway.

The science teacher looked up and down the hall. The coast was clear. He was the only one there.

He walked over to the shelf where the science projects were displayed. And he made his way over to the cave. He looked up and down the hall once more to be sure nobody was around. Then he reached his right hand into the cave.

Travis had done a nice job of securing the tin of water to the floor of cave. It looked quite natural—and it took the science teacher much longer than he expected to free the tin of water from the clay floor. The man took his time, not wanting to spill any of the precious water.

The science teacher's plan was a simple one. He'd remove the tin of water from the cave and empty the water into a glass jar on his desk. Then he'd place a lid on the jar, screw it shut, and bring the jar to a laboratory. The laboratory would analyze the water and provide him a report listing the contents of the water. Once he knew what it was in the water that had the mysterious healing power...he would sell the information to a major pharmaceutical company—and become rich. No more teaching for him.

The man was daydreaming of early retirement as he carefully removed the tin of water from the cave. He cautiously carried the tin of water across the hallway and brought it back to his classroom. The glass jar was on his desk, just like he had planned. Everything was perfect. He had all the time in the world. All he had to do now was empty the water into the jar. After that, he'd refill the tin with tap water and place it back inside the cave. Nobody would ever know.

Mr. Calcuttu set the tin down on his desk with great care. Then, he unscrewed the lid from the jar and placed the lid on the desk. He then lifted the tin from the desk ever so carefully. The man was a bundle of nerves. There was big money at stake here. The guy's hands were shaking and water was splashing in the tin. He was almost there though. He raised the tin over the glass jar.

"Excuse me, sir!"

The science teacher dropped the tin. It landed upside down on his desk. Water splashed over the papers on his desk and cascaded onto the floor...There wasn't a drop of water left in the tin.

The janitor was hovering in the doorway. "Uh, I didn't mean to startle you, sir. I saw your light on. Just wanted to let you know I'm here to empty the wastebasket."

The science teacher said nothing, just stared at the mess on his desk. He was too spellbound to speak. A fortune had just slipped through his fingers.

Mr. Calcuttu didn't sleep that night. His mind was racing. He lay awake in bed thinking about the water. The precious water. He had been so close. So close to the deal he'd been waiting for, the deal that would make him rich—and allow him to sleep late every day for the rest of his life.

The hours ticked by and still he could not sleep. His mind was still racing. But then, just before three o'clock in the morning, an idea came to him. A simple, wonderful idea. All was not lost after all. He would just ask Travis where the cave was. The boy was sure to tell him. That's all there was to it. He would go to the cave himself to get the sample of water that he needed. It would be a piece of cake. Mr. Calcuttu smiled. The guy's mind was suddenly at ease and he finally drifted off to sleep.

Chapter 16

When Travis arrived for seventh period science the following day, Mr. Calcuttu approached him again. "Travis, how are you, boy?"

"Uh…good, thanks."

"I'd like to talk with you a bit more about this cave. *Where* did you say the cave was located?"

"I don't think I did mention where the cave is located."

"Well, it's local, correct? You mentioned it's here in Eastborough?"

Travis shook his head yes.

"Wonderful. I was thinking the class could take a field trip to see it. We'll be doing a segment on stalactites and stalagmites in a few weeks. It would be a nice learning opportunity for everyone."

Travis shook his head no. "There are no stalactites or stalagmites in the cave, sir."

The science teacher frowned. "Well, that's okay. It would still be a good learning experience, I'm sure."

Travis sighed. "Uh, the location is not really appropriate for a field trip, sir. It's real hard to reach."

"Please, Mr. Macgregor, we're talking about suburban Massachusetts—not some off-the-grid location in the boondocks. If you've been there, I'm sure your classmates and I could make it there without a problem."

Travis looked at the man. "It's in a rough, hard-to-get-to spot. I was fishing when I found it. I was wearing old clothes, not school clothing."

Brriiiiinngg!

Mr. Calcuttu cursed. It was time to teach. Teaching was such an interruption. The only thing he wanted to do now was devise a plan to find the cave. Travis Macgregor was being tight-lipped about the location. But there had to be a way to locate the cave. The science teacher just needed some time to come up with a strategy.

*****

71

The nursing coordinator called Travis over when he arrived at the nursing home later that afternoon. "Do you have a minute?" she asked.

"Sure." Travis walked over to the front desk.

As he neared, the nursing coordinator said, "Just a heads up. There's a group of folks waiting to talk to you—"

"There he is!"

Travis glanced down the hallway. A dozen residents were headed toward him. Some were pushing walkers. A few were in wheelchairs; others were slowly advancing up the hallway unassisted.

The nursing coordinator glanced at Travis. She flashed a smile. "I tried to warn you."

"What do they want?"

"I think you're about to find out."

The crowd approached the front desk. And an elderly woman stepped forward. "Hello there, young man. How are you today?"

"Fine, thanks...are you folks looking to subscribe to the paper? I can bring some extra papers tomorrow."

An old man wheeled forward in his wheelchair. He was clad in bed clothes, but his attire was more formal than that of those around him—a retired businessman, Travis guessed. "We don't want the paper, son. What we'd like is some of that water we've been hearing about!"

"You heard about the water I brought Mrs. Calhoune and Mr. Baskis?"

"Indeed we did!" the man said.

"That's right," someone shouted from the back of the crowd.

"Absolutely!" another person in the crowd chimed in.

It was clear that the group was united—they all wanted some of the water.

Travis raised his hands and said, "Okay, okay. I'll bring you folks some water."

"Yaay!"

"Yippee!"

"Bless you!"

Travis couldn't help but smile. He would be glad to venture back to the cave for these people. He would go to the cave on Saturday.

*****

Mr. Calcuttu thought long and hard all week. He had to find the cave and that's all there was to it. But how? By Friday, he still hadn't come up with anything. He paced around his apartment for a few hours when he got home on Friday afternoon. Then he took a brief break for his TV dinner. After dinner, he began pacing again. Around eight o'clock, he stopped pacing momentarily to feed his pet turtle.

The turtle peered at him through the aquarium glass, from its island in the center of the aquarium. Six inches of water surrounded the island. As Mr. Calcuttu placed the turtle's food on the island, it suddenly hit him. *Water.* That was the key to finding the cave. Travis had told him he'd discovered the cave when he was fishing. He just needed to find out where a boy would go fishing in Eastborough.

The man eagerly spread a map of Eastborough out on his kitchen table. There were no ponds or lakes on the map—but there was a river that cut through the southern portion of town.

That's it! This is going to be easy.

Chapter 17

Mr. Calcuttu woke up far earlier than usual on Saturday morning. He fed his pet turtle, grabbed a cup of coffee for the road, and headed out the door. He drove to the southeastern edge of town. But he didn't spend much time there. The river cut through the mill district in the southeastern section of town. Not much chance of finding a cave there.

He headed west on River Street. The street paralleled the river as it meandered through the business district. Then, after the business district came suburbia—blocks of single family homes with tidy lawns that ran to the river's edge.

Mr. Calcuttu continued west on River Street. Five minutes later, shortly before the town line, the landscape transitioned to fields and then the fields gave way to woodland. The only place to pull over was a small dirt parking lot beside a canoe launch on the left side of the road.

The science teacher pulled his old sedan into the lot. Then he got out, stretched his back and looked the area over. To the left of the boat launch area was a grassy spot with two picnic tables. Beyond that was a meadow. No chance of a cave there.

He diverted his attention to the area to the right of the boat launch. Thick woodland. There was a muddy trail leading into the woodland. It was several yards in from the riverbank and appeared to parallel the river.

Mr. Calcuttu walked over to the trail. He looked down into the mud at the beginning of the trail. There were two sets of footprints—one set going into the woods and one set coming out. They were not large footprints like those from an adult. But they weren't from a child either. Mr. Calcuttu guessed they were made from a size 8 shoe—the size that Travis Macgregor likely wore. *I'm on the right path. It won't be long now.*

The man started making his way down the trail. Less than thirty seconds later, he was up to his ankles in mud. The guy cursed himself for wearing tennis shoes—new tennis shoes. From there, the trail only grew worse. It began to narrow and the woodland closed in on the trail; branches brushed the science teacher at every turn.

The man forged on and a few minutes later the trail disappeared at the edge of a swamp. Beyond the swamp was more woodland. The swamp was dotted with clumps of marsh grass.

The science teacher wasn't an outdoorsman. He didn't understand that he could keep his feet dry by jumping from one clump of marsh grass to another. He walked into the swamp…and soon he was up to his knees in mud.

The man cursed again, louder this time. The only good news was that there was the promise of dry ground in the woodland beyond the swamp. When he finally cleared the swamp and made it to the woodland, he found another trail, but this trail wasn't as perceptible as the previous one. And this section of woods was full of green briers. Thorns ripped into the science teacher's pants and tore his windbreaker as he made his way down the trail into the woodland.

Five minutes later, the briers became even denser. Thorns cut the science teacher's face, neck, arms, and hands as he moved through the growth, the trail nearly imperceptible now.

The man continued on until he could no longer see any sign of the trail at all. He looked all around him. But all he saw were ferocious briers and trees. Not being an outdoorsman, the man knew nothing about tracking.

The cove was just fifty yards away when the science teacher turned around and gave up in frustration to begin the long, treacherous trek back to the boat launch ramp. When he was halfway through the swamp, he tripped on a root and fell face-down in the muck. The science teacher cursed louder than ever.

Back at the boat launch ramp, a family—a mother, father, and a young girl—was eating lunch at one of the picnic tables. The girl heard a rustling noise. She looked over at the trail that emerged from the woods. And she screamed.

"Swamp Monster!"

The mother and father looked over. There was a man standing on the trail at the edge of the woods. He was covered in mud. And his clothing was in shreds. The man did indeed look like a *swamp monster*.

The family watched as the swamp monster slowly walked over to his car, got in, and drove away.

"Swamp monsters can drive?" the girl asked her parents.

Her father shrugged. "Apparently so."

Chapter 18

Travis stifled a yawn as he entered the nursing home on Saturday afternoon. It had been a long day. His delivery bag was strung over his left shoulder and in his right hand he carried a large bucket of water— water that he had obtained from the pool in the cave that morning.

The nursing coordinator walked up the hall to greet him. She smiled when she saw the bucket of water. Some of the water had spilled during the trek back from the cave but not much. "You're going to make a lot of people very happy," the woman told him. "This is mighty nice of you, Travis."

Travis smiled. "It's nothing."

"Oh, but it is...Everyone is waiting in the entertainment room."

"I'm on my way."

"I'll give you a hand."

"Thanks."

There were a dozen residents in the entertainment room. Each one of them appeared anxious. When Travis entered the room, someone shouted, "He's here!" The entertainment room was suddenly buzzing with excitement.

"Good to see you, boy!"

"Thanks for bringing us the water!"

"I sure could use some of that water!"

"Me too!"

"Over here, son. I'll take some of that water."

The nursing coordinator raised her hands. "Okay folks." she said with a smile. "There's plenty of water to go around. Everybody will receive a share."

"How should we do this?" Travis asked her.

The nursing coordinator thought for a moment. Then, she said, "Hold on. I'll be right back."

The crowd gathered around Travis. Some people patted him on the back. Others shook his hand. And some just smiled and watched anxiously from the perimeter. All were grateful.

The nursing coordinator returned a few minutes later. She was carrying a ladle and a dozen pie tins.

She set the tins and the ladle down on a table at the center of the room. Then she motioned to Travis to place the bucket of water on the table.

"Okay folks, one at a time," the nursing coordinator said. "There's more than enough water to go around."

Chapter 19

Sylvia Boutweile was a reporter for the *Eastborough Times*. She was at the nursing home visiting her grandmother. The two of them were just returning from a walk when they heard a commotion in the entertainment room. Curious, they made their way down the hall and entered the entertainment room.

"Oh, my!" Sylvia's grandmother exclaimed. "I almost forgot about the *water*. I've got to get some!"

"Water?" Sylvia asked.

"That's right. *Special* water."

Sylvia Boutweile's eyebrows rose. "What's so *special* about the water?"

"It has healing power," her grandmother whispered. "It's therapeutic."

Sylvia listened as her grandmother told her how Iris's hands had been healed by the water. And she continued to listen as her grandmother told her about Burt Baskis's elbow being healed by the water too. She glanced to the center of the room where a boy was ladling water into tins at a table. The nursing coordinator was distributing the tins of water to residents who anxiously waited their turn in line. There was an excitement in the air. Everyone was chatting away.

Sylvia looked around the room. On the far side of the room, and elderly lady was soaking her hands in a tin of water. Beside her, another woman was splashing water over her forearm. And a man at the opposite side of the room removed the slipper from his right foot and dipped his foot into a tin of water.

Sylvia didn't know what to make of it. But one thing was for sure. This was newsworthy. There was a story here.

*****

When Travis stepped into the nursing home on Monday afternoon to deliver Iris's paper, the place seemed unusually quiet. Usually, he could hear the entertainment room's television down at the front desk. But not today. He made his way down the hallway.

When Travis passed by the entertainment room, he glanced inside…The room was empty. *Strange.*

There were always people in the entertainment room. This was a first.

He continued down the hallway. The nursing coordinator was walking up the hallway toward him.

"Hello, Travis."

"Hi...where is everybody?"

The woman smiled. "Follow me."

Travis followed the woman to the east wing. Once there, she turned into the cafeteria. Travis followed her inside.

On the cafeteria's far wall was a large picture window that overlooked the grounds at the rear of the property, including a patio and a small pond that was encircled by a walking trail.

The nursing coordinator pointed at the picture window. "Look outside."

Travis looked through the window. And he was stunned at the sight before him.

A half dozen residents were practicing yoga on the patio. Burt Baskis was out on the patio too. He was holding a tennis racquet. The man appeared to be giving tennis lessons to several residents. Iris, Eleanor, and several others were playing croquet on the back lawn. And a few residents were walking around the pond. One guy was even fishing in the pond.

"This is amazing," Travis said.

"It's all you're doing," the nursing coordinator smiled.

"Huh?"

"They've been active like this ever since you delivered that water last weekend."

You're kidding?

Chapter 20

Travis's mother had just sat down at the kitchen table to enjoy a cup of coffee before heading off to work on Wednesday morning. That day's edition of the *Eastborough Times* was on the table. And the bold headline on the front page caught her attention:

Water Delivery at Riverview Nursing Home Is Cause for Celebration

When Travis stepped into the kitchen a few minutes later, his mother smiled. She got up and hugged him. Travis noticed that her eyes were misty.

"I'm so proud of you, kiddo," she said.

"Huh?"

His mother handed him the paper. "Congratulations, sweetheart. You're front page news!"

The bold headline was hard to miss. Travis sat down at the table and began to read…

A recent water delivery at the Riverview Nursing Home has caused quite a stir. This wasn't your typical water delivery, where a delivery truck pulls up out front with bottles of water for the water cooler. This water was delivered by a paperboy—and he carried the water in a bucket...

The article went on to tell about how the residents of the nursing home claimed the water was therapeutic and made them feel years younger. There were several quotes from Iris, Burt, and a few other residents. The words "fountain of youth" were mentioned. And the story carried over to the second page, where there was a picture of a dozen nursing home residents holding tins of water, all of them grinning.

*****

Mr. Calcuttu had been out on Monday and Tuesday that week. A substitute teacher filled in for him on those days. But he was sitting at his desk reading the paper when his first-period students arrived on Wednesday morning. The students sat down in their

88

assigned seats. They couldn't see the teacher's face; the paper was screening their view.

Brriiiiinngg!

The science teacher sighed. There was no getting around it. It was time to teach—time to face the students. He lowered the paper…and exposed his face.

"Aaagh!"

A number of students gasped. A few girls shrieked. And a kid at the back of the room said, "Ouch!"

The science teacher's face was laced with scratches. There were scratches on his nose, forehead, cheeks, and chin. And there were scratches on his neck too. The man had apparently been cut as well; there were three band-aids on his face. And his hands were scratched up as well. Every student in the class stared at him.

It's going to be a long day.

Mr. Calcuttu was the first to arrive in the teacher's lounge for lunch that afternoon. He pulled his lunch from the refrigerator and brought it over to the table at the center of the room. Someone had left the

Wednesday issue of the *Eastborough Times* on the table. The science teacher was just biting into his baloney sandwich when the headline on the front page caught his eye. He began to read...

*****

Later that afternoon, when Travis stepped into the classroom for seventh period science, Mr. Calcuttu walked over to him. He gave Travis a friendly pat on the back as if
they were best buddies. "Mr. Macgregor, how are you doing?"

Travis winced at the sight of the scratches and band-aids on the man's face. "F-fine. Thanks."

"That was an interesting article in today's paper. Did you read it?"

"Uh...yeah."

"Good thing you did—bringing the water to those folks at the nursing home. A good thing indeed."

"Thank you, sir."

Mr. Caluttu had that desperate look in his eyes again. "So, are you planning to visit the cave again to get more water?"

"Yes, I'm going there on Saturday. I'm going to bring some more water to the nursing home this weekend."

The science teacher smiled. He had the information he needed. He was back in the game.

Chapter 21

When he was walking up Pleasant Street on his way home from school that afternoon, Travis noted a large white van just up the street. It was parked along the curb. There was a satellite dish mounted on the van's roof. As he neared, Travis observed it was a news van...and it was parked directly in front of his house.

There were two people standing in front of the van—a middle-aged, heavyset man and an attractive woman who Travis guessed was in her twenties. When he reached the front walk to his house, the two of them approached him.

The man was wearing jeans and a faded t-shirt. The woman was clad in formal attire—a red blouse and dark dress pants. She had dark brown eyes and long blond hair that was pulled back into a tight ponytail. The woman was wearing makeup, but Travis didn't think she needed it. She extended her right hand.

"Hello, I'm Geni Gastao, with KBHG News. Are you Travis Macgregor?"

"Uh…yeah."

Geni Gastao smiled. "I'm glad we were able to catch up with you."

"Huh?"

"I'd like to talk with you—about the water you delivered to the Riverview Nursing Home last weekend. The story in the *Eastborough Times* caught our attention today."

"Sure."

"Great! We'd like do a segment for the evening news. We think people will be interested to hear your story and learn more about the water you delivered to the nursing home."

"Um…could we wait until my mother comes home?"

Geni Gastao flashed another award-winning smile. "Absolutely. I wouldn't want it any other way."

*****

Mr. Derek Jaccobie was eating dinner at his parent's home in Eastborough that evening. The man

93

had just arrived from New York City that afternoon. His parents had recently retired and moved to Florida. The man was working with a local real estate agent to sell the house and had returned to his childhood home to tidy it up for an open house that weekend.

It had been challenging to steal away from work that day. Nothing new there. As vice president of acquisitions for Brook Trout Pharmaceutical Inc., the man had little free time.

Derek Jaccobie turned on the television just in time to catch the evening news. There was a shot of a news van parked on Pleasant Street. He recognized Pleasant Street. It was only two streets over from his childhood home. Back in his youth, he had played countless games of street hockey in the lot at the lower end of Pleasant Street.

An attractive twenty-something woman was talking into a microphone. *"An article in today's Eastborough Times caught our attention. The article focused on a local paperboy who made a special delivery to residents at the Riverview Nursing Home last weekend. And we decided to investigate..."*

*****

Travis and his mother were cleaning dishes at the kitchen sink, talking nonstop about Geni Gastao's story on the evening news. Then the phone rang. Mrs. Macgregor picked it up.

"Hello...Yes...Yes...Oh...Yes...Um...Wow!... Sure...That will be fine. We'll see you then."

Travis glanced at his mother as she hung up the phone. There was a surprised look on her face.

"What's up, Mom?"

"We're going to have a visitor tonight...An executive from a pharmaceutical firm in New York."

"What does this person want?"

Just then, a dark sedan with New York plates pulled up to the curb in front of the house.

"I think we're about to find out..."

Derek Jacobie stepped out of his late-model sedan and headed up the front walk to the Macgregor home. It had been years since he'd been in the old neighborhood. The last time he was on Pleasant Street he had been wearing sweats, street hockey equipment and old tennis shoes. Now he was wearing wingtips and a three-piece suit. The man was a modern day success story. He had worked long hours, making his way up the corporate ladder in the years since graduating from business school.

Derek Jaccobie knocked on the front door. A boy came to the door and opened it. The kid looked to be of middle school age.

"You must be Travis."

"Y-yes."

The man extended his right hand. They shook hands. "I'm Derek Jaccobie. I spoke with your mother tonight, told her I'd stop by. I'd like to talk with both of you if you have some time."

Just then, Mrs. Macgregor stepped into the room. "Hello, Mr. Jaccobie."

"Good to meet you, Mrs. Macgregor. Thanks for not minding the intrusion at this hour. I promise to brief."

"No problem at all. Please come in."

Travis looked at his mother. "What's going on, Mom?"

"Mr. Jaccobie has some business he'd like to discuss with us."

"Huh?"

"That's right, Travis." The man confirmed.

Mrs. Macgregor motioned toward the living room. "Let's sit down. Can I offer you anything to drink, Mr. Jaccobie?"

"Please, call me Derek. And yes, a glass of water would be great if you don't mind."

"Sure thing. Be right back."

Travis glanced at Derek Jaccobie as his mother headed into the kitchen. "What is it that you want to talk to us about?" he asked.

The man smiled. *"Water."*

Derek Jaccobie didn't get right down to business. He was a humble man and the guy seemed to enjoy talking about the old neighborhood and the days of his youth. He had attended the same schools as Travis. And it turned out the two of them had a lot in common. The man was a fisherman too. He had fished the river often in his youth.

He did eventually get down to business though, told Travis and his mom that the story on the evening news had caught his attention. Derek Jaccobie mentioned that if the water that Travis discovered could in fact heal certain ailments, it would very likely be of interest to his company. And he told them that if that were the case, there would be money involved—potentially, a *lot* of money.

Travis gulped when he heard the news. His mother glanced around the living room, took in the worn furniture and the faded drapes. She looked out the window at her rusted fifteen-year-old sedan in the driveway. They could sure use the money. If anyone could use money, it was the Macgregors.

Derek Jacobie asked Travis if he had a sample of the water. Travis shook his head no, told him he would be going back to the source to get more water on Saturday.

"I'll be leaving town tomorrow morning," Derek Jaccobie, informed Travis and his mother. "I've got a business trip coming up. But I'll be back in town the week after next. Travis, if you could arrange to get me a sample of that water when I return, I'll bring it to our lab in New York so they can get the research underway and have an analysis done. After that, we'll talk business. What do you say?"

Travis nodded yes. "I'll have the water for you."

Mrs. Macgregor said, "We look forward to seeing you upon your return Mr. Jac—er, Derek."

"Likewise," Derek Jaccobie said, as he shook hands with each of them and bid them goodnight.

*****

From the stares and glances Travis received in the hallways at school the following morning, it was apparent that people had seen the news the night before, or had at least heard about it. It was as if he had achieved some type of instant celebrity status overnight. Kids he didn't know, girls included, said, "Hey Travis" as he passed by them in the hallways.

Later that morning, when he cut through the science wing on his way to the cafeteria for lunch, a crowd of students and teachers was gathered around his science project in the hallway outside Mr. Calcuttu's classroom. Everybody was anxiously waiting for their turn to take a look inside the cave.

Travis was the talk of the school at lunch. It wasn't a bad thing, he thought. In fact, the attention felt good. But school wasn't the only place where he received attention that day.

When Travis got home that afternoon, there were a dozen messages on the answering machine—messages from organizations and companies he had never heard of before: venture capitalist firms, pharmaceutical companies, and bottled water distributors.

The phone rang that night too. His mother screened the calls and informed callers that Travis was not available and for them to leave their name and number.

The following day, Friday, was basically a repeat—except Travis received even more stares and greetings from students in the hallways at school. And there were even more messages on the answering machine when he got home from school that afternoon. One guy—a rather aggressive salesman—even knocked on the door during dinner that night.

Chapter 22

Mr. Calcuttu woke far earlier than usual on Saturday morning. He fed his pet turtle, filled a thermos with hot coffee, and headed out the door. The sun was just starting to rise; he could see his breath in the cool morning air as he walked out to his car.

The man drove across town to River Street. He followed River Street through the business district and then through the suburban stretch that wound through neighborhoods of single family homes and fields, before reaching the wooded section just before the town line.

He pulled into the small dirt parking lot and parked his sedan beside the boat launch. Then he killed the engine, turned the lights off, and slid down in his seat until his eyes were level with the dashboard. After that, he poured himself a cup of coffee from the thermos. And then he waited for Travis Macgregor to arrive.

Travis pulled his Schwinn into the lot an hour and a half later. There was a bucket dangling from his bike's handlebars. The kid removed the bucket from the handlebars and ditched the bike in a thicket to the right of the boat launch. Then he picked up the bucket and headed down the muddy trail into the woodland.

Mr. Calcuttu got out of his car and quietly shut the driver-side door. Then he walked across the lot to the trail that Travis had followed into the woodland. The man was wearing newly-purchased hip boots, briar-proof camouflage pants and a matching jacket. The safari hat on his head completed the outfit. He had purchased the apparel the night before at Eastborough Sporting Goods. The price tag had been hefty, but he thought of the purchase as an investment. Soon, there would be plenty of money.

The science teacher tightened the chin strap on his safari hat and headed down the trail into the woodland. He followed Travis's footprints. Travis's footprints were clearly visible in the mud at the beginning of the trail, but from his previous experience, the science teacher knew that wouldn't be the case for long. He made his way down the trail as fast as he could. And he was soon up to his ankles in mud, thankful for the newly-purchased hip boots.

He needed to catch up to Travis and keep the boy in sight before he reached the section of woodland where the briers obstructed all visibility. If he wasn't close behind Travis when the kid reached that spot, he knew he wouldn't be able to stay on his trail and find the cave.

Thankfully, Travis was wearing a red wool jacket. Mr. Calcuttu caught a glimpse of him up ahead, as he made his way through the swamp. When Travis cleared the swamp and entered the woodland beyond it, Mr. Calcuttu was close behind him, but not too close. He emerged from the swamp and he followed Travis into the woods. And he didn't let Travis out of his sight when he reached the dense briers that had defeated him last time.

The science teacher was only fifty yards behind Travis…when he tripped over a root. The science teacher landed face-down on the forest floor. And when he stood up a few moments later and regained his balance…Travis was gone. There was no sign of the kid. It was as if he had vanished. Mr. Calcuttu cursed as he jogged to the area he had last seen Travis.

All he saw when he reached the spot though was briers.

The man peered into the dense growth. The guy couldn't see more than fifteen feet ahead. *How could the kid just disappear?*

He looked all around for an opening in the massive wall of briers. There was no opening…except for a faint deer trail. *He couldn't have made his way through the briers on that trail?*

The science teacher stepped onto the deer trail, brushed the briers away as best he could, and slowly moved forward on the thin trail. Thorns tore into his face, neck, and hands as he advanced through the briers. Then, up ahead, he saw a flash of red. *I'm on the right path! It won't be long now.*

Travis continued down the deer trail as it meandered through the briers. He reached the cove in record time. From there, he headed north—toward the ravine behind the cove.

Once again, the sounds of machinery could be heard in the distance. The sounds grew louder as he neared the ravine.

Travis reached the bottom of the ravine five minutes later. And then he suddenly stopped. Everything was different. The slope of the ravine had been completely filled in with boulders and rocks. Hundreds of tons of boulders and rocks. Travis was wonderstruck.

A few moments later, the whine of a diesel engine could be heard above the ravine. And then a bulldozer was pushing soil over the edge of the ravine. Tons of soil. It cascaded down the ravine, seeping into the crevices between the rocks and boulders.

The cave was gone. Gone forever. It had been completely filled in and now lay under hundreds of tons of boulders and rocks.

"So, where is it?!"

Travis was stunned by the voice. He was even more stunned when he turned around and saw who was staring at him.

"Mr. Calcuttu?"

The science teacher was a wreck. His clothing was caked in mud. The man was sweating profusely and breathing heavily. There were fresh scratches on his face, neck, and hands. A thin trail of blood ran down his forehead from a gash at his hairline.

"Where is it?" the man repeated. The guy had that desperate look in his eyes again.

"Where's what?" Travis replied.

"The cave! The cave with the *magic water!*"

Travis sighed. "It's gone. Gone forever."

"What do you mean it's *gone*?!" Tears welled in the science teacher's eyes.

Travis pointed up at the boulder and rock-covered slope above them. "It was up there."

Just then came the whine of a diesel engine from above the ravine. And then a bulldozer was dumping a load over the edge of the ravine. This time the load wasn't soil, but rather boulders—tons of boulders which were now rolling downhill toward them.

Travis looked at his science teacher and yelled,

"RUN!"

Chapter 23

Travis sighed when he pulled up to the Riverview Nursing Home later that morning. The residents there were eagerly looking forward to more water, he knew.

Hopefully, they still have enough water left to last them a while.

The nursing coordinator smiled when she saw him enter the nursing home.

"Good morning, Travis!"

"Morning."

"Everyone is anxiously waiting for you. They're out back on the patio. I can't thank you enough for what you have done, Travis. That water has been a game changer here...Did you bring more water?"

Travis sighed. "There's no more water...The source is gone."

The nursing coordinator's eyebrows lifted. "Oh my."

Travis stared downward. "I was actually hoping there might be some water left over. I'm in need of a sample of it."

The woman shook her head no. "I'm afraid it's all gone."

"Gone?"

"Yes…Someone from the corporate office paid us a visit yesterday. They were concerned the water would be unsanitary after use…so they instructed us to empty everyone's water tin. I'm so sorry."

Tears welled in Travis's eyes. He thought of his mother. She deserved an easier life. That easier life had seemed so close just yesterday; it had been within reach.

"You should be very proud of what you have done for everyone here, Travis."

"T-thanks."

Travis couldn't bear the thought of breaking the news to the residents at the Riverview Nursing Home. But there was no getting around it. He slowly made his way outside to the patio.

"He's here!" someone shouted when Travis neared the patio.

The crowd was buzzing with excitement. But things quieted down quickly when people saw the look on Travis's face—and observed that he wasn't carrying a bucket of water this time.

"Hi everyone...I'm very sorry to say...there is no more water," Travis informed the group. "The source is gone."

There were a few sighs and some of the patrons looked suddenly distant. But then Burt stood up and said, "Well, it was good while it lasted."

"It surely was," Iris agreed. And then others joined in.

"Easy come, easy go."

"I'm glad I was able to get a bit of it."

"Absolutely!"

"We shall survive."

"Thank you, Travis!"

"Yes, a big thanks to Travis!"

"Hip, hip, hooray!"

It wasn't what he was expecting. Travis was surprised by how the residents took the news in stride. They appeared to be thankful just to have had a chance to benefit from the water for a brief time. These were people who had lived through world wars, rationing, economic depressions, and other hardships after all.

Travis felt a little better when he left the nursing home...but there was a heavy feeling in his stomach. He just needed one measly sample of the water. The nursing home had been his last hope.

Chapter 24

The phone calls continued the following week. And each day when Travis got home from school he found letters in the mailbox. Letters from venture capitalists, pharmaceutical firms, water distribution services, nonprofit businesses and other organizations. Travis sighed when he read them. Each phone call and letter was a reminder of lost wealth. How close he and his mom had been to a life where utility bills, car repairs and other expenses would not be a concern. A life in which his mother wouldn't have to worry about working extra hours to make ends meet.

The phone calls subsided later that week as Travis and his mother informed the callers that there was no more *magic water*, never would be. And the letters trickled out too. But reality really hit home the following week when they broke the news to Derek Jacobie. The dream of a better life was officially over.

*****

Travis shivered when he walked into the kitchen for a glass of juice on the third Saturday of December. His mother had set the thermostat on low to save money. She was sitting at the kitchen table, dressed in her nursing uniform. His mother was sifting through bills. Travis saw the words *Final Notice* on more than one bill.

"Morning, Mom. How come you're dressed for work? It's Saturday—your day off."

His mother looked up at him. Her eyes were puffy and her cheeks were wet. She had been crying.

"Hey, kiddo."

"What's wrong, Mom?"

His mother sighed. "Things are just a little tight financially, sweetheart, particularly now that the heating season has arrived. I picked up some extra hours at the hospital. I'll be working Saturdays from now on. Not to worry, we'll get by."

"We will," Travis assured her. "Bye, Mom. I'm off to deliver the papers."

"Have a good day, sweetheart…Oh, I'll be late coming home from work…The car won't start. I'll be taking the bus to and from work for a while."

"Sorry, Mom."

*****

Travis ripped his jeans when he hopped over a barbed wire fence on his paper route that day. His mother saw the tear when he got up to wash his plate after dinner that night. "I'll get my sewing kit and patch your jeans," she said. "We can't exactly afford new pants right now."

"Thanks, Mom."

Travis changed into sweats and brought his mother the torn jeans a few minutes later. His mother opened up her sewing kit. She sifted through the scraps of fabric inside it for a patch. She found a piece that was a close match and removed it from the kit. When she placed the patch over the tear however, she saw that it was too big.

"Sweetheart, could you get me a pair of scissors? I need to trim this patch."

"Uh…the scissors are broken, Mom."

"Oh, that's right."

Travis thought for a moment. "I have a real small pair of scissors that I use to cut fishing line."

"They'll do."

"They're in my fishing vest. I'll go get them. Be right back."

Travis went out to the back hall. His fishing vest was hanging on the hook, right where he left it after his last fishing trip at the end of the summer. He lifted the vest...It was heavy. Too heavy to hold just fishing tackle. And then he remembered...The water bottle. The water bottle he had filled with water from the pool in the cave. It was right there in the front pocket of his vest.

"Mom!"

"What?"

"You're not going to believe this..."

Chapter 25

One Year Later…

"We'll be touching down in sunny Aruba in twenty minutes," the pilot announced. "The temperature in Aruba is currently a balmy eighty-five degrees."

Travis smiled. It had been snowing out when his mother pulled her new SUV into the airport parking lot that morning. He glanced over at his mother in the seat beside him. She was asleep. And she was smiling.

After years of watching other people take vacations, they were finally able to take one themselves. Travis glanced out the window. He stared at the endless expanse of blue ocean below. And his mind drifted back over the course of the last year…

Derek Jaccobie had been quite pleased to learn about the forgotten water bottle that contained water from the pool in the cave. Upon hearing the news, the man drove out from New York City to pick up the bottle of water at the Macgregor's home. And true to his word, the Macgregors soon had more money than they had ever had before. Brook Trout Pharmaceutical Inc. was quite generous after their laboratory identified therapeutic minerals in the water.

Travis's mother no longer had to worry about money. She and Travis were all set financially. Bills and car repairs were no longer a concern. And they had money put away for Travis's college education. Their future was secure.

Mrs. Macgregor no longer had to work. Now she *volunteered* at the hospital. And though Travis no longer delivered papers, he still made deliveries to the Riverview Nursing Home—water deliveries that is. Brook Trout Pharmaceuticals Inc. gave him a lifetime supply of *magic water*.

Printed in Great Britain
by Amazon.co.uk, Ltd.,
Marston Gate.